MW00965301

THE STORYTELLER AT FAULT

THE STORYTELLER
AT FAULT

DAN YASHINSKY

ART BY NANCY CAIRINE PITT

RAGWEED
THE ISLAND PUBLISHER

Text Copyright © Dan Yashinsky, 1992
Artwork Copyright © Nancy Cairine Pitt, 1992
ISBN 0-921556-29-2

To Nathaniel and Jacob

Cover Art: *Ali the Persian's Bag*
Editor: Lynn Henry
Design: Catherine Matthews

Distributed in Canada by:
        GENERAL PUBLISHING
              30 Lesmill Road
              Don Mills, Ontario M3B 2T6
for
        RAGWEED PRESS
              P.O. Box 2023
              Charlottetown, Prince Edward Island
              Canada   C1A 7N7

Printed and bound by:
        Wing King Tong Co., Ltd., Hong Kong

CANADIAN CATALOGUING IN PUBLICATION DATA
        Yashinsky, Dan, 1950–
              The storyteller at fault
              ISBN 0-921556-29-2
        I. Pitt, Nancy Cairine, 1933– II. Title.
        PS8597.A74S76 1992   jC813'.54   C92-098630-7
        PZ8.1.Y37St 1992

Once upon a time a king went blind. His son set out to find a cure and rode so far he left his father's kingdom far behind. One day a golden feather lay blazing in the prince's way, and when he bent to pick it up he heard his horse speak up and say: 'Don't touch that feather, my friend, for it will bring you fearful trouble. That is a feather from the shining wing of the Firebird herself ...'

— SAVE THE FILE! SCRIBE, SAVE IT AND PRINT IT! GUARDS, TAKE HIM AWAY!

— What's going on, your Majesty? Where are your guards taking me? What is making that awful sound?

— That is the sound of your death, Storyteller. My scribe is printing out your stories. All these nights while you were speaking, my scribe was hiding in the shadows with his special machine. It is a machine for memory, Storyteller, and unlike you, it will *never* forget these stories. As you said the words out loud my scribe keyed them into his database. Now the memory machine will keep them safe and never let them be forgotten. Listen well, Storyteller: that sound is a thousand nights of word-of-mouth turning into hard, hard copy.

— Hard indeed, your Majesty, if it means the teller himself must die. Have mercy on me!

— Stand up, Storyteller. Take courage from your own stories. In all of the tales you told me, not one hero or heroine ever begs for their life. Get off the floor!

— Those heroes and heroines lived in fairy tales that always ended happily ever after. I'm a real person, a living man with a wife to love and children to raise. I know that one day I will have to die; but not tonight! I'm not quite ready, your Majesty. I'm really a bit too young to die ...

— GUARDS!

— But why is this night different from all our other nights together, your Majesty? Why tonight must I die for my stories?

— Because tonight, Storyteller, you have come to the end of your own memory. Tonight you began to tell me the story of the Firebird. That is the first story my scribe entered in your file, a thousand nights ago. You have no more stories to tell, and so you must die.

— But your Majesty, the first time I told it to you, I remember well my hero was a young archer. Tonight I said he was a prince.

— Details, details. I'm sure they both ride forth to discover a radiant destiny. It is the same story, even if you change the names of your characters. No, Storyteller, you have come back to your own beginning. TAKE HIM AWAY!

— At least tell me my crime, your Majesty. What is the true reason for this dreadful judgement?

— I will tell you the truth, Storyteller. When I first listened to you I was enchanted by your tales of wonder. You used the same words as everyone else, but in your mouth those common words turned to pure gold. Your voice could conjure distant lands, fabulous treasures, yes, even the beauty of the Firebird herself. But one day the spell was broken. I grew afraid that your precious stories would be forgotten, would vanish into breath and dust and be lost without a trace. I was so afraid that I commanded my scribe to invent a machine to save your stories from oblivion. He caught your stories with his memory machine and locked them into chips of glass and gold. Now they will never unravel, or lose their colours like a carpet left out in the rain. Now they belong to me.

— But now that you have captured the words from my very lips, surely his Highness can spare the life of his humble storyteller ...

— No, tonight you must die. You see, Storyteller, as my hoard of stories grew larger, my fear turned into anger. I was outraged that you, of all people, could be so heedless with your priceless tales. You cast them forth by word of mouth, like flower petals thrown on a fast river. One day even your mighty memory would loosen its hold, losing a word here, a word there—until finally all would be forgotten.

— I will *never* forget my stories!

— Yes, Storyteller, one day you would betray your own stories. I condemn you to death not because I hate your stories but because I love them all too well. You are at fault for the crime of forgetfulness you would inevitably commit. At least you will die knowing that your stories will outlive you. Guards!

— Your Majesty ... there is one more story. It is my secret story. If I perish tonight my story will die unheard. Would you have the death of a story on your hands as well as the blood of a storyteller? ... Please ...

— Storyteller, you may tell me one last story. Then my guards will take you away. Scribe, reopen his file.

— You are merciful, your Majesty. The name of my story is *The Last Story*.

THE
LAST STORY

Once upon a time there was a father who loved to tell stories to his little boy. Every night he'd go into the boy's room, sit on the bed, and tell him fairy tales. One night the father was about to begin when the little boy turned away. He buried his face in the pillow and pulled the blanket over his head. The father could hear the little boy breathing hard, close to tears.

"How about a story?" the father asked.

The boy burst out crying and said something that surprised his father very much: "No, Daddy, I don't want to hear any more stories."

After awhile the tears slowed down and the father peeled the blanket down a bit. He put his hand on the boy's shoulder and said, "What's up? How come no more stories?"

The boy was still turned away when he whispered, "I hate fairy tales. They're not true."

"Not true?"

"Yeah. They always end happily-ever-after and that's not true. There's no such thing as a happily-ever-after ..."

The father sat for a time in the dark room. Then he said, "Remember a couple of days ago you kids found the dead robin in the yard? You dug a hole by the apple tree and buried it in a shoebox. We were watching you from the kitchen window. Is that dead bird still on your mind? Is that why you don't want any more happily-ever-afters?"

The boy nodded into his pillow.

"Well," said the father, "that's a riddle, alright, maybe the hardest one in the world. A bird is alive and flying around, doing loop-de-loops, stealing flower seeds, making a nest; then it's dead. You bury its body but then you wonder what happens to the rest of it. Whatever is in a bird to make it fly, where does that part go? I don't know the answer to that riddle, but I do know a story about it. The story's called *Tortoises, Humans and Stones*. I don't think I've ever told it to you before. You want to hear it?"

The boy nodded and the father began:

A long time ago, in the beginning of the world, Worldmaker made all the living creatures and all the things of the earth. In those days Worldmaker made all the living creatures so that they could live forever and they never had to die. But there was one condition: they could not have children. One day two tortoises, male and female, came to Worldmaker and said, "There's a problem with the world you made. We want to have children now."

"But if I let you have children, you'll have to start dying. Otherwise there'd be too many of you."

"If we can first look upon the faces of our children, we will be willing to die."

Then two human beings, a man and a woman, came to Worldmaker. They too said, "We would like to have children."

"Are you willing to die?"

"Yes, Worldmaker, we are willing to die."

12

And so it was that tortoises and humans and all the living creatures chose to have children, even though they had to begin dying.

And that's how the story says death came into the world.

"What about the stones, Daddy?" said the little boy. "You said there were stones in this story."

"Yes, the stones ... Well, the stones never wanted to have children. That's why stones never have to die."

Now the boy turned to his father and said, "How old are you?"

"I'm forty-one."

"Is that old?"

"Well, it's older than you and younger than your grandfather. Why do you ask?"

The little boy didn't answer for awhile; then he said, "You can tell me fairy tales again, Daddy. But I still don't want them to end happily-ever-after. Do you know any other kind of stories?"

"Sure I do," said the father. "I know lots of stories. How about I tell you ten stories, and I promise that not one of them will end with the words happily-ever-after? Tonight's story of the *Tortoises, Humans and Stones* can be the first, and tomorrow night I'll tell you the second, and so on until we have ten stories. Deal?"

The boy nodded, and his father kissed him, turned out the light and closed the door.

*The following night, the father told the little boy
the story of*

THE DREAMER
AND THE BUTTERFLY

This is a true story. My grandfather told me it happened to two friends of his, when they were all soldiers fighting in a big war.

The two friends had been separated from their company during a battle, and they had spent the day walking through the fields trying to catch up. It was a quiet, sunny day, peaceful after all the shooting. The two men walked into a lovely meadow and decided to have a little picnic. They found a creek in the middle of the meadow, dipped their cups in it, and drank the cool, fresh water. They sat in the long grass at the end of the meadow and munched their K-rations. Then, feeling a bit sleepy, one of the soldiers stretched out to have a short nap.

The other man stayed awake. He looked at his friend's face and saw an amazing thing. The moment his friend fell asleep, his mouth opened and a pale blue butterfly came out. It rose into the air above the sleeper's head, fluttered here and there as if trying to decide on the right direction, and finally began to fly across the meadow.

The friend got to his feet and followed the blue butterfly. It flew slowly and close to the ground, and was easy to keep up with. The butterfly approached something white that gleamed in the green grass. The soldier saw that it was a skull—what kind of skull my grandfather never told me—and a crowd of flies and bees swarmed in and out of the sockets. The blue butterfly landed on the skull and folded its wings and walked in. The buzzing increased inside the skull. After a little while the butterfly came out again and resumed its flight.

It flew towards the little stream of water that wound through the meadow. When it reached the stream it flew this way and that way, but didn't fly across. The man laid his rifle over the water and the butterfly flew across. On the other side of the stream it flew to a small mound of earth at the far end of the field. It disappeared into the mound. Finally it came out again, flew back across the meadow, over the water, past the skull, and hovered over the face of the sleeping man. His friend watched with astonishment as the butterfly dropped to the sleeper's mouth, folded its delicate blue wings, and disappeared.

At that moment the sleeper awoke. He yawned and stretched and shook his head. He looked at his friend and said, "What a strange dream I just had. If only I could have what I just dreamed about!"

"What did you dream?" asked his friend.

"Well, first I dreamed I was walking and I came to a great palace made of white marble. I entered the gates of the palace and met many lords and ladies dressed in fine clothes. They were singing and talking, and they greeted me warmly. I stayed with them for a long time, but then I felt it was time to leave. Although they begged me to stay with them, I left their palace. I then came to a great river, too wide to get across. After much searching I found a bridge that

16

spanned the river and I crossed to the other side. Then I travelled for a long time until I came to a huge hill. There was an entrance on the side, and I walked in. I saw at once that it was an ancient tomb, a royal burial mound. In the middle of the tomb was a leather sack, and inside the sack I found a great treasure. But just as I tried to take the precious things out of the bag I woke up!"

His friend listened very carefully to the dream. Then he said, "Follow me," and he led the dreamer through the meadow, past the skull, over the stream, and up to the small mound at the far end of the field. "Dig here," he said.

The dreamer knelt down and brushed the dirt away and found a soldier's helmet. He picked it up and turned it over. There were two things inside: a gold watch and a photograph. The man wound the watch and found that it was still working. He looked at the photograph. A young woman and a little boy were smiling and waving good-bye.

"How did you know about this helmet?" the dreamer asked his friend.

His friend told him about the blue butterfly, and the dreamer was amazed. They never did find out whose helmet it was. The dreamer kept the gold watch, and his friend kept the photograph of the woman and child.

On the third night the father told the little boy
the story of

THE

GREEN MIST

A long time ago people believed that everything in the world was alive—the water and the earth and the weather. Everything had its own spirit.

In those days people would go out into their fields in late autumn and sing lullabies to the earth, preparing it for the long sleep of winter. When winter came they bided close to home. They were afraid the spirits of the earth grew restless in the long, cold nights. For protection, they would carry a light all around their homes before turning in for the night. And they'd always be sure to leave a bit of bread and some salt out by the threshold to keep the spirits from going hungry. As winter neared its end, the people would go out into their fields at dawn, turn over a clod of earth, and recite the strange, ancient prayers they had heard from their grandparents. They would pray for the Green Mist to rise up from the ground and signal the beginning of spring.

There was a certain family back then who had endured a long and bitter winter. The worst of their troubles was that the daughter of the family, a lovely, tall teenager, had taken sick and was getting sicker by the day. She had wasted away during the winter and now, near winter's end, she had barely the strength to lie beside the window and gaze out at the patches of snow. She would lay there all the day long, watching for a flash of cardinal's red, or a show of green buds, or any sign of spring at all.

"Oh, Mother," she'd say, over and over, "if only I could wake the spring with you, the Green Mist might bring my strength back to me, like it brings strength to the flowers and the corn and apple trees."

And her mother, working, mending, cooking the girl's broth, would look at her lying there and look away, shaking her head.

Spring was late coming that year, and the girl was failing fast. She grew as pale and wan as a snowflake melting in the sun. She knew now that she'd never be able to go out into the fields with the others to dig up the clod of earth and wake the spring. "At least," she said to her mother, "at least take me to the door for the prayer, and I'll put out the bread and the salt."

"Yes, my daughter," answered the mother, "I promise."

And every morning the people went out to see if the earth had wakened; but winter still lay white and heavy on the land.

One day towards nightfall, as the house filled with shadows, the girl turned away from her window. She watched her mother for a long while, her eyes open and unblinking. Then she said, "If the Green Mist doesn't rise tomorrow I shall never see it again. The ground is calling me, Mother, and the seeds are bursting that will one day bloom over me. Oh, if only I could see the spring wake once more, I swear I'd be happy to live as long as one of the cowslips by the gate—and to die with the first of them at season's end."

"Hush, daughter," whispered the mother, bending to the

hearth, "you shouldn't make such strange wishes."

But the very next morning the Green Mist did rise, and the land was filled with the fine, soft scent of spring. The snow melted quickly and the buds appeared and the seeds sprouted and the air smelled sweet and new. The mother and father carried the girl to the threshold and she crumbled the bread and salt and cast it forth, into the garden. She murmured the old welcoming prayer and her parents, holding her, said the words with her, slowly and quietly. Then they put the girl back to bed and she slept for a very long time. She dreamed of yellow sunshine and bright wildflowers.

Soon the cowslips bloomed and the girl came back to life. Each day she found more health and vigour until she was able to leave her sickbed and run out to the garden. Her parents stood at the window and marvelled to see her running in the sunshine. She stopped at the gate and gazed down at the pretty primroses. Then she walked among the flowers and held her head and hands up to the great, golden sun, as if she lived only in its warmth.

And so the days passed. On sunny days she would be in the garden, dancing and joyous; on cloudy days, though, when the sun was hidden and the weather was cool, she stayed indoors near the fire, shivering and white.

The garden was in full bloom now, and the girl could not leave her flowers alone. The people were astonished to see the girl lively and beautiful again. They often came around to watch her at her gardening, to look at her graceful, young body bending to tend the flowers, to listen to her singing. Her mother, though, worried sometimes and scolded sometimes: "You're out here too much, daughter, too much ... and maybe I'll pull the flowers up, to make you leave them!"

"Leave them be, Mother," the girl would reply, "leave them be—they'll be fading soon enough by themselves."

One day a boy from the village stopped at the gate to have a chat. He was talking to the girl's mother and he bent down and picked a cowslip. The girl joined them and saw the flower in the boy's hand. "Where did you pick that cowslip?" she asked, never taking her eyes from it.

"From beside your own garden gate," said the boy; then, noticing her loveliness, he said, "I picked it for you." He held the flower out to her and she took it from him.

The girl held the flower in her hand. She looked at it for a long time. Then she looked at the handsome lad, and at her mother. She looked at the garden and the apple trees, and the ripening fields. Then she looked up at the bright, burning sun itself. She gave a high, strange cry. Then she shrank away from the light as if it scorched her; and she turned and ran back into the house.

She never rose from her bed again. She held the pretty, pale flower and watched it fade and wither, and she faded with it. By nightfall she was dead—a wilted, broken thing, laying beside the window. Her mother took the flower from the girl's hand and kissed them both, the girl and the cowslip.

The people around there said afterwards that the spirits of the earth had heard the girl's wish. They had let her bloom with the early spring flowers, and die with the first of them.

THE TRUE FATHER OF THE HOUSE

Once there was a traveller who was walking down a lonely road. He didn't know where he could stay the night, and it was getting darker and darker as he walked. Luckily, there was a big farmhouse down the road; and huge it was, looming like a castle out of the darkness. The traveller hastened towards it thinking he'd find room there, and hospitality for the night.

When he came up to the front door, he saw an old man chopping wood. "Good evening, father," said the traveller, "I'm out on the road tonight and I'm in need of shelter. Have you room in your house for a traveller?"

The old fellow put down his axe and answered, "I'm not the father of this house. You'll have to go inside and ask my father. Go into the kitchen. You'll find him sitting by the fire."

The traveller opened the massive farmhouse door and walked into the kitchen. In the kitchen was a great stone fireplace, and in front of it on his hands and knees was a very old man trying to blow on the embers of the fire. The traveller came near him and said, "Good evening, father. Can you put me up for the night?"

The old man looked up from the sparks and ashes and replied, "I'm not the father of the house. Go into the parlour and ask my father. He is reading at the table."

When the traveller came to the parlour he saw a very, very old man sitting at a table and reading a book. He barely had the strength to turn a page, and each page that he turned raised a cloud of dust. The traveller spoke up: "Good evening, father. Can you give me shelter in your house tonight?"

The old man raised his eyes from the ancient volume. "I am not the father of the house," he said. "You had better ask my father. He's sitting on the sofa smoking his pipe."

The traveller noticed a shape bundled up in blankets and sweaters. Two thin hands poked out of the blankets, one holding a pipe and the other a match. The hands shook so that the pipe could not be lit. The traveller walked over and held the match steady. The old man on the sofa lit his pipe. The traveller said, "Good evening, father. Is it possible for me to stay in your house tonight?"

In a voice as thin as the blue pipesmoke the old man answered, "I am not the father of the house. Go ask my father. He is resting in bed."

The traveller passed into the bedroom of the house. There was a bed, and in the middle of the bed was a small bump. When the traveller bent over he could see that the bump was a very, very old man. He was so old and wizened that only his eyes seemed to have any life in them. They were open and luminous. The traveller looked at those eyes and repeated his request: "Good evening, father. Can you put me up for the night?"

"I'm not the father of the house," came the reply. "You'd best go ask my father. He's lying in his cradle."

There was a cradle in the bedroom. The traveller stepped over

26

to it and looked inside. A man lay there. He was so old that he was no bigger than a baby. His beard curled around him like a wispy blanket. Except for a wheeze that rattled up from time to time there was no way to tell if he was alive or dead. "Good evening, father," said the traveller, "and have you room in your house for a lonely traveller this night?"

It took a long time to get an answer and the answer, when it came, took a long time coming. "I," the old man wheezed, "am not"—the voice was as dry as a leaf in autumn—"the father of the house. Go ask my father. He is hanging in the horn upon the wall."

The traveller now saw a great hunting horn hanging upon the wall. Slowly, very slowly he approached it. He peered within and saw something there—white as ash and tiny: a human face. The traveller now cried out, "GOOD EVENING, FATHER. CAN YOU PUT ME UP FOR THE NIGHT?"

The voice that came from within the horn was as light as a tomtit chirping. The traveller strained to hear what it said, and what it said was this: "Yes, my child."

Then a table appeared, laden with delicacies and fine wines; and when the traveller had eaten, in came a bed all covered with soft reindeer-hide blankets. The traveller curled up to sleep, and just before he closed his eyes he thought to himself: it is good to find the true father of the house.

THE BIRD COLOUR-OF-TIME

Long ago, back in the time when kings and lords tried to run things, there lived a certain king, and he had an only daughter. She was next in line to rule the land if her father the king quit or died.

One day the princess fell gravely ill. For a long time she stayed in bed, and nobody knew whether she would live or die. Finally, just as this story begins, the princess was starting to feel a little better. One fine spring morning she got out of her sickbed and went to see her father. She walked into the court, past all the lords and ladies and royal guards, and marched right up to the king's great throne. She had a big favour to ask of him.

"Father," she said (she never called him "dad"), "there's something I want you to give me. Just as I was starting to feel better I had a dream. I dreamed I met the fastest bird in the world. Can you find it and bring it to me?"

"What kind of a bird was it?" asked the king, a little worried by his daughter's strange request.

"It was a little bird, the colour of time," she said.

Now, the king had heard of bluebirds, blackbirds, goldfinches, yellowhammers, cardinals, hummingbirds, and hawks. But he'd never heard of the Bird Colour-of-Time. "What colour is that, exactly?" he asked. "Is it white or black or clear or the colour of rainbows?"

"Dunno," said the little girl, "It's just its own colour. I only saw its tail-feathers. It's very fast! Can you get it for me, Father?"

The king was not amused. He had no idea where to look for such an extraordinary creature. Besides, truth to tell, the king was a little frightened of strange birds. He knew that a man could be tickled to death by even one feather—especially from a bird the colour of time, he thought. This king didn't like the idea of dying laughing—or dying any other way, for that matter. So he stalled for time. He hemmed and he hawed, he stared at the ceiling, he gazed at his shoes, he pulled his earlobe, he cracked his knuckles, he whistled "God Save the King," he peeked over at the big clock ticking on the palace wall ... and still his little daughter stood before him, waiting patiently for his reply.

Finally an idea popped into the king's head. A flying contest, he thought; that's how we'll see who's the fastest birdie of them all.

No sooner thought than done. The king organized a grand affair, the *World's First Speed Flight Competition for Birds*. It was to be a truly spectacular sporting event. The Royal Treasurer spared no expense. Invitations were sent by passenger pigeons to every bird for miles around. Each species was invited to send its speediest flyer.

On the appointed day the racers gathered at the starting line, which was the border of the king's realm. The rooster gave the signal (he and the hen weren't in the race) and with a loud COCKETY CROW! the birds were off and flying. They rose and raced across the sky in a vast cloud of every colour and hue, each one straining to fly higher and faster than the rest, passing overhead with a terrific beating of wings and piping of birdcry.

For a time they were all racing beak to beak; but then, all of a sudden, the mighty Eagle pulled ahead. He soared towards the finish line, leaving the rest far behind. The majestic, the one-and-only Eagle was a sure bet to win.

The king looked up and thought: "What a fine, what a strong, what a *kingly* bird—*c'est magnifique*!"

But the little girl watched the race and shook her head. "That's not the one," she said to herself. "That's not the bird I saw in my dream."

The Eagle glided forward, taking his sweet time, as if he had all the time in the world to cross the finish line.

Then something happened. Just before the Eagle reached the end of the race, a tiny bird that had stowed away in the great bird's neck-feathers shot forward and flitted ahead and crossed the line— winning the race by the beat of a wing.

The princess leapt to her feet and yelled, "That's the one, that's the one!" But the king was furious. It was outrageous, it was a scandal! That regal bird losing the race to such a disgraceful little hitchhiker! There was tumult, there was commotion—and in the uproar the winning bird disappeared. Only the little girl saw where it went, and nobody asked her, and she never told.

The magnificent Eagle was so embarrassed by his loss that the feathers on his head turned completely white. They have stayed white to this very day. He flew away to his own country and became a recluse, always roosting in the highest mountains and brooding on his shame. To console him for his defeat, people turned him into a symbol for victory. Now you can find his picture on flags and shields and government buildings.

As for the little girl, she was happy. She was healthy again and, as time went on, she grew up. At the proper time, she became a wise and well-loved queen. People used to tell stories about the Great Flying Contest and, as more and more stories were told, people agreed less and less about what had really happened so many years before. Some people claimed that the winning bird was nothing but an ordinary wren—a common, everyday sort of a bird out to have a lark with the proud Eagle. Other people said no, it wasn't a wren, it *was* a lark. The only thing they all remembered was that *something* had flown by awfully fast; something had won the race at the very last moment.

Whenever she heard her people talk, the queen would smile to herself. She knew who had won the race. For there's only one thing that can outrace eagles, only one thing in the world so swift. Sometimes you see it in a fever-dream, sometimes as a season wheels past, and sometimes at the edge of an ordinary sky, glanced at and gone. All you ever really see are the tail-feathers as it flashes past. It is the little bird, the fastest of all, Colour-of-Time.

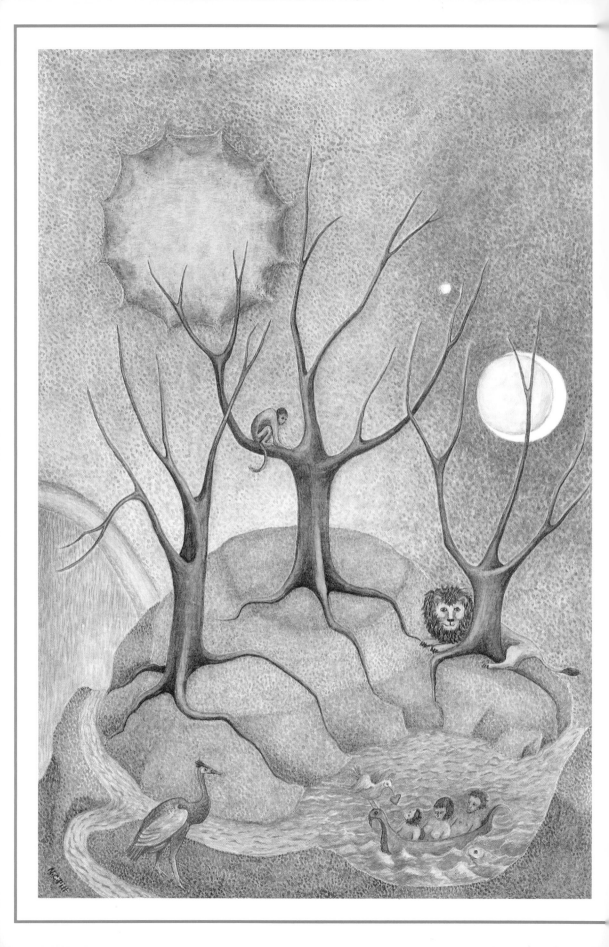

On the sixth night the father told his son
the story of

HOW HEART CAME INTO THE WORLD

A long time ago, in the beginning of things, Worldmaker made the world. Worldmaker made the earth and stars and water and creatures. Man and Woman were given intelligence but they did not possess Heart.

One day Worldmaker called Sun, Moon, Darkness and Rain and said, "My children, I have almost finished making the world. Soon the time will come for me to leave. I am going to send Heart in my place. Before I leave you, my children, I would like to know what you plan to do when I have gone. You, my bright Sun, what will you do?"

Sun answered, "Worldmaker, I will become hotter and hotter, and shine upon the Earth with all of my strength!"

Worldmaker spoke to Sun and said, "No, my child. That is not a good idea. You would burn the world with your heat and dazzle it with your brightness. No, Sun, here is what you must do. Take turns with Rain. After you warm the Earth, let Rain come and refresh it. That is the proper way to be. And you, Rain, what did you have in mind?"

"Oh, Worldmaker, I want to pour and pour and pour upon the Earth, and cover it with my waters!"

"No again, my dear one. If you flood the Earth, all the creatures will be swept away. Instead, take your turn with Sun. You will cool and water the Earth in the proper season, and Sun will warm it again. How about you, Darkness, what do you intend to do?"

"I want to rule forever!" shouted Darkness.

"Child, this cannot be. If you ruled forever the creatures of the Earth would not be able to look upon the loveliness I have made for them. No, Darkness, you will rule only when Moon is in its last quarter. Only then will you have your dominion. And as for you Moon, my sweet, strange child, the night will be yours to shine in. Sometimes you will shine full and round, sometimes you will make a thin crescent of light. Up and over you will go, cutting loose dreams. So it will be forever, my children. But my time has come to leave you, and this world that I have made. I will send Heart in my place."

So saying, Worldmaker disappeared.

Not long afterwards Heart came into the world. Heart was small and red, about the size of my fist. Heart was crying. Heart came to the children of Worldmaker and said, "I am looking for the one who made me. Tell me where I can find the one who made this world."

Sun, Moon, Darkness and Rain replied, "We do not know where Worldmaker has gone. We do not know where you must search."

Heart said, "I long to meet the one who made me, but since Worldmaker has gone away, I will enter into Man and Woman. Perhaps through them I will find the one I seek."

And so, ever since then, every child of Man and Woman has been born with a longing to meet the one who made the world. And that is what we call Heart.

*On the seventh night the father told the little boy
the story of*

THE MASTER OF THE TEA CEREMONY

Long ago in Japan there was a master of the tea ceremony. This teamaster practised his art in the palace of Lord Tosa.

One day Lord Tosa was invited to visit the Shogun in the city of Yeddo. He brought with him not only his warriors but also the master of the tea ceremony. He wanted the Shogun to enjoy his teamaster's great art.

The custom of the Shogun was that every man who entered his palace should be dressed in the traditional costume of a samurai warrior. When the teamaster arrived with Lord Tosa's entourage he too began to wear the two crossed swords of a samurai, although he had never before worn a sword in his life.

On many occasions in the next few days Lord Tosa asked his teamaster to perform the tea ceremony, and the teamaster became a favourite of the lords and ladies of the Shogun's court. After a few days, the teamaster was given leave to spend a few hours out in the streets of the city. He was delighted to leave the palace and wander about, watching the hustle and bustle of the marketplaces, hearing the cries and laughter of the children.

When it was time for him to return to the palace, the teamaster began to walk back the way he had come. He came to a bridge and began to cross it. Coming towards him on the bridge was a large, mean-looking man. This man was a *ronin*, a free-lance mercenary who roamed the countryside, sometimes serving an honest cause but more usually making trouble for law-abiding citizens. The *ronin* was in an ugly mood. As he passed the little teamaster he jostled him so that he fell to the ground. When the teamaster stood up and tried to walk away, the *ronin* stopped him and said, "How dare you push me and knock me around!"

"Pardon me," said the teamaster politely, "but I believe it was you who knocked against me. I was the one who fell."

"Are you calling me a liar?" the big man shouted. He hadn't failed to notice that the teamaster was short and slight of build. "Come on, take out your sword and let's settle the argument right here and now!"

"Ah, I'm afraid that I cannot oblige you with a fight," said the teamaster. "Let me explain. You see, I'm not really a samurai. I practise the tea ceremony for Lord Tosa. I am wearing these garments and swords because my lord is visiting the Shogun, and I must dress like a warrior to enter the palace. I have never held a sword in my life."

"So you say," the *ronin* sneered, "and what I say is that you are nothing but a coward. If you refuse to give me satisfaction, if you refuse to fight, I will tell the whole town that your Lord Tosa is served by men who have no honour."

The teamaster had no wish to bring dishonour to his lord. He stood before the *ronin*, his mind racing and his heart pounding. All of a sudden he had an idea. He remembered that on his meander through Yeddo he had passed an academy of swordfighting. He thought to himself, "I will return to that academy and learn at least how to hold the sword properly; then when he kills me I will not die in a shameful manner."

He spoke to the *ronin* and said, "I will fight you. Before I do so, grant me two hours to complete a certain errand. I promise to meet you back here on the bridge and settle our dispute with swords."

The mercenary thought that the little man must be going off to collect a bribe, and he was happy to grant the delay. "See that you return in two hours," he said, "or all of Yeddo will know of your disgrace."

The teamaster hurried down the street to the door of the swordfighting academy. He explained breathlessly his urgent need to see the swordmaster, and the doorman brought him in. As quickly as he could, the teamaster described his dilemma, concluding, "... so you see I have come to learn from you how to hold a sword properly so that when I receive my deathblow, at least I will die with honour."

"I understand," said the swordmaster. Then he smiled.

"What's so funny?" asked the teamaster. "I myself find nothing amusing in the situation."

"Pardon my smile," said the swordmaster. "Most of my students come to me to learn how to avoid death, and how to bring death to their enemies. You are the first man who has ever come to me to learn the art of dying."

"Do not mock me!" cried the teamaster. "Please teach me what I need to know."

"Before I teach you my art," said the swordmaster, "would you be so kind as to show me yours?"

The teamaster knew that this would be his last chance to practise his art. With a great effort he began to prepare. He assembled the elements and utensils of the tea ceremony: the tea, the water, the whisk, the clay vessel, the brazier. Then he prepared himself. When all was ready, with a peaceful spirit he was able to serve the tea to the swordmaster.

The swordmaster observed the teamaster carefully and, after he had sipped from the bowl of tea, he said, "I see now that you are already a great master. I have nothing further to teach you. You already know everything necessary for your combat. Let me just make one suggestion. When you return to the bridge for the fight, approach your enemy as if he is a good friend. Go to him as if he is your most honoured guest at the tea ceremony. When you arrive, be sure to greet him politely and thank him for waiting for you. Take off your jacket, roll it, and place it on the ground. Place your fan upon it. Roll up your sleeves. Tie the headband of resolution around your forehead. Face your opponent. Grasp your sword by the hilt, draw it, and hold it above your head. Announce your readiness for his attack. Then close your eyes. When you hear his battle cry, bring your sword down with all your strength. If you do exactly as I say, I assure you that all will be as you desire. Farewell—and have a good death."

The teamaster was puzzled by this strange advice. But there was no more time for a lesson in swordfighting. He thanked the swordmaster and took his leave. He began to walk back to the bridge. As he walked, he felt calm, as if he were about to practise the tea ceremony for a well-loved friend. Step by step he approached the scene of the combat.

The *ronin* was striding about, shouting and brandishing his sword. A crowd had gathered, eager to see blood. The teamaster walked slowly up to the *ronin*, greeted him, and thanked him for waiting. He placed his jacket and fan upon the ground, rolled up his sleeves, and tied the headband of resolution about his head. He took his sword, held it above his head, and said that he was ready to fight. Then he closed his eyes.

He had no tea. He had no water. He had no whisk. He had no clay vessel. He had no brazier. The only thing left to offer was himself.

The teamaster stood there for a long time.

The *ronin*'s cry of attack did not come. Finally the little man opened his eyes. The *ronin*'s sword lay on the ground in front of him. As for the big mercenary, the teamaster could see him running away down the street.

When the *ronin* had looked at the face of the teamaster, he had lost his nerve. He did not know how to fight an enemy who showed neither hope nor fear. He saw the teamaster standing peacefully, eyes closed, sword held without a quiver high above his head, and he was terrified. He threw his own sword down and ran away, glad to escape with his life.

The teamaster picked up his things and returned home. Before leaving Yeddo he visited his friend at the swordfighting academy. He served the swordmaster tea and told his story, and the swordmaster smiled again.

On the eighth night the father told his son
the story of

THE
SILENT PRINCE

Once there was a king and a queen and they had a son. As he grew older, this little boy became strange and silent. By the time he was a teenager he had altogether quit talking. And so he became known as the Silent Prince.

The prince's parents were desperate with worry. The queen never gave up hope that her son might become normal, but the king was sure his son was terribly damaged. When the prince was almost eighteen years old, the king and queen had an idea. They issued a proclamation that said: "Whoever can make the Silent Prince speak will win a great reward." In fine print at the bottom of the proclamation were the words: "Whoever tries and fails will have his or her head chopped off."

Despite the dire consequences, many brave men came and tried to win the great reward, and many brave men had their brave heads chopped off. Whatever they said to him, whatever they tried, they always failed; the prince could not or would not speak.

Down the road from the palace lived a young woman with her grandmother. One day the girl said to her grandmother, "Granny, I would like to try to make the Silent Prince speak."

"That is not the cleverest thing you have ever said, granddaughter. Do you not know the punishment for failure?"

"Yes, granny, I do. But you are a wise old woman. You've spent time in the forest, you know the powers of herbs and flowers, you've read many books, you know many poems by heart. Please teach me what you know, granny, and perhaps I'll have a chance."

And so the grandmother said to her granddaughter, "Very well. I will teach you my wisdom on one condition. You must listen to me all night and not interrupt once."

The girl agreed and the grandmother began to speak. It wasn't easy, listening for such a long time, but the girl did. In the morning, her grandmother finished speaking. "I have taught you my wisdom," she said, "and the rest is up to you. Good luck, my beloved."

She kissed the girl, and the girl set off towards the palace. When she arrived, she told the guard she wanted to go in. He led her before the king and the queen, and she told them that she'd come to make the Silent Prince speak.

"Here are the rules," said the queen. "You will spend the night with our son in his bedroom—with a witness. In the morning the witness will tell us what he saw."

The girl went into the prince's bedroom and sat down. She didn't say anything at first, and this surprised the prince very much. All of the men who had come to make him speak had done all of the talking. The girl just sat there. The prince looked at her. He thought she was very beautiful. Finally, the girl began to speak, but not to the prince. She turned to the witness and said, "Tomorrow I am going to die. Could you tell me a story that would lighten my heart and prepare me for my death?"

"I'm sorry," said the witness, "but I don't know any stories. I'm just a witness."

"Would you at least listen to my story if I told it to you?" she asked.

"Yes, I'll listen," said the witness.

The girl began:

There were three women once and each had a special power. One of them had a telescope, and when she looked through it she could see anything that was happening anywhere in the world. The second woman had a magic airplane, and she could travel instantly to anywhere in the world. The third woman had lived for many years in the forest and knew about herbs and healing plants. She'd found an apple tree that grew special apples: one bite could cure any sickness. The three women were good friends, and one day they met and began to show each other their gifts and powers. The first one looked through her telescope and said, "My friends, I see a palace on the other side of the world, and in it a young man is dying." The second one said, "Get on board my airplane and we'll go there right now." They travelled instantly to that palace. The third woman, the herbswoman, went to the young man's bed and offered him a bite from her magic apple. The young prince was instantly cured. He leapt from his sickbed and saw three beautiful young women in his bedroom. He thought to himself, "I'm healthy now, and I'm single. I'd like to ask one of them to marry me."

And here the girl stopped her story and said to the witness, "I have a question for you. Each one of the women did something to make the sick prince well. Which one did the most? Which one should he ask to marry him?"

The witness answered, "I don't know. I'm not very good at riddles."

But the prince had been listening very carefully and he said, "I have an idea."

"I'm very pleased to hear you say that," said the girl. "What is your idea?"

"I think he should ask the young woman with the apple. The one who used her airplane lost nothing by using it; the one who used her telescope lost nothing by using it. But the woman who gave up a bite of her apple will never get that bite back again. She is the only one who gave up something for the sake of the sick prince."

"A wise answer, O prince," said the girl. "May you also one day find someone who is willing to give something up for you."

In the morning the king and queen came in and asked the witness what had happened during the night. He was very pleased to be able to tell them that the Silent Prince had finally broken his silence. The queen was over the moon with joy. "Thank God," she cried, "I knew he could speak!"

But the king didn't believe it. "Why," he said, "should my son start speaking now, just because a beautiful young woman spent the night in his room? I insist on a second night with *two* witnesses!"

So that night the girl was in the room with the prince and two witnesses. Again she sat for a long time and did not say a word. Finally she turned to the two witnesses and said, "My friends, tomorrow I will die. Will you tell me a story to give me courage and make the night pass pleasantly?"

"We're not storytellers," they said, "we're just witnesses."

"Would you at least listen to my story if I told it to you?" she asked.

They agreed to listen and the girl began:

There was a young girl who lived in a village, and she was a witch. She was very much in love with a young man, but she never told him she was a witch. She was afraid he would leave her if he found out the truth. One night the young man was walking alone in the woods, and up ahead he saw a witch. He picked up a large stone and threw it at her. She turned to escape, but the stone caught her on the back of the leg. The next day when the boy went to visit his girlfriend he noticed she was limping. When she turned around he saw that there was a wound on the back of her leg, in the same place he'd thrown his stone. He said, "So it's you ... you're the witch!" And she admitted everything: "Yes, I am the witch."

The girl stopped her story and said to the two witnesses, "I have a question for you. Now that the boyfriend knows the truth about his lover, what should he do?"

"We don't know," they said, "we're not very good at riddles."

The prince had been listening very closely to the story, and he spoke up. "I have an idea," he said.

"I am very pleased to hear you say that," the girl replied. "What is your idea?"

"I think he should marry her, and they should keep her secret together."

"A wise answer," said the girl, "and an unusual one for a man. Many men would have said—she is a witch; drive her away; burn her. But you understand that when people love each other, not only do they give up their secrets, they learn new ones as well. May you also find someone who will give up a secret for you."

In the morning the king and queen came in and asked the two witnesses what had happened, and both of them said, "Your Majesties, last night your son spoke!" Again the queen was overjoyed; but the king still didn't believe it. "I insist on one more test," he said, "with *three* witnesses."

And so the same thing happened for a third night. The girl, the prince and the three witnesses sat together quietly for a long time. Finally the girl turned to the witnesses and said, "Please, my friends, tomorrow I face my death. Tell me a story that will help me get through the night."

"We have no stories," they all said.

"Would you listen to my story if I told it to you?"

They agreed to listen and the girl began:

Once there was a man who dreamed of firebirds. One day when he was in the woods there was a great flash of golden light. He hid behind a tree and closed his eyes. When he dared to look he beheld a beautiful woman taking off a suit of golden feathers and stepping into a pool to bathe. He gazed at her loveliness. Then he reached forth and stole her golden feathers and hid them away. When the woman came out of the pool she searched for them but could not find them. The man came out of his hiding place and said, "Come with me and I will give you shelter." The woman knew that she could not fly away and so she followed the man through the woods to his house. He had a good house, and he was gentle, and she stayed with him. One day she gave birth to a child, a little boy. She loved her son very much. The boy was about five years old when he came running to his mother, one day when his father was away. "Mama," he cried, "I was playing in the woods and I found something pretty! Come and see!" The woman went with her little boy. They came to a tree, and there in a hollow place she found her golden feathers, blazing with their golden light. She picked them up and went back to the house with her son. She sang him lullabies and put him to sleep. With one hand she stroked the little boy's hair, and with the other she held her golden feathers.

And here the girl stopped her story and said, "I have a question for you. Now that the woman has found her feathers again, what should she do?"

The three witnesses shook their heads. "We don't know," they said, "that is the hardest riddle of all."

But the prince had been listening very carefully and he said, "I have an idea."

"I am pleased to hear you say that," the girl said. "What is your idea?"

"I think that it is not up to me to judge the woman of your story, nor can I judge the man. Your story is both bitter and sweet at the same time. If I were the man in your story, and could see the firebird in her true form, I think that I too would do anything to keep her with me. And if I, like the woman, had once come from the sky, I think that I would never lose my desire to return to it."

"A wise answer, O prince," said the girl. "Some stories are not meant to be judged, but only to be heard and remembered. The woman kissed her son, stepped outside, put on her golden feathers and flew away. When the man returned, the woman was gone."

"And what happened to her little boy?"

"Some people say that he cried for his mother until he lost his voice and became silent. Others say that when he awoke he found a golden feather shining on his pillow, and this feather brought him luck and joy and courage and love for the rest of his life."

In the morning the king and queen came in and the three witnesses all agreed: "Last night," they said, "your son spoke!" The queen was jubilant and the king also believed them. He turned to the girl and said, "Now that you have done what all those men failed to do, what would you like as your great reward?"

And now, for the first time, the girl was silent. She had not been thinking about her reward, but only about her stories. The prince rose and walked towards her. He took her by the hand and lifted her up and looked her in the eyes. "Choose me," he said.

And the girl said, "I have an idea. I'll take him!"

So it was that they were married. It was a grand celebration. In the seat of honour was the girl's grandmother. She was holding a big bouquet of wild herbs and flowers she'd picked that day in the woods. As the girl walked by, the grandmother handed her the flowers and said, "You see, you should always listen to your granny!"

ALI THE PERSIAN'S BAG

Long, long ago there lived in the city of Baghdad a mighty Caliph named Haroun al-Rashid. He loved to walk through the streets of his own city in disguise, peering in through garden gates, eavesdropping at secret windows, listening to the stories his people told. But he had trouble sleeping at night. One night as he tossed and turned he called his vizier Jafar and said, "Jafar, my heart is heavy. Find some way to lift my spirits."

"I hear and obey without delay," said Jafar. "I happen to have a friend known as Ali the Persian. He is a renowned storyteller, and if anything can lift a troubled heart it's a good story. I will bring him to you."

When Ali the Persian came before the Caliph he bowed and said, "Your Majesty, would you like to hear a story about something I heard, or something I saw with my own two eyes?"

"Tell me the truth," said the Caliph.

"Very well," said Ali, "I will tell you of something that

happened to me the other day: I was standing in my shop in the marketplace when I noticed a man from Kurdistan come in. He looked at this and he looked at that, and finally when he thought I wasn't looking, he picked a bag off the shelf and walked out without paying for it. I followed him into the street, seized him by the sleeve and began shouting, "Shoplifter, shoplifter! Give me back that bag!"

"Never!" he cried. "This bag is mine. Yesterday someone stole it from me, and today I found it in your shop!"

We began to quarrel and a crowd gathered around us. They took us to the courtroom of the local cadi, the district judge, who looked at us both and said, "What is the cause of this dispute?"

"This bag is mine," I said, "and this fellow stole it!"

"No, no!" said the Kurd, "the bag is mine and I found it in this man's shop."

The judge said, "For me to come to a proper judgement, you will each have to tell me what the bag contains."

"I can tell you what it contains," said the Kurd, "because it's my bag. It has—

a silver jar of eye-shadow

two make-up brushes

a candlestick

and two lemonade glasses with gilded rims

and a waterpot with two ladles

and a small carpet with two matching cushions

plus a pregnant cat

a jar of rice

two sacks of wheat

a bedroom suite

a female bear

a racing camel

a canopy

a kitchen with two doors

and a company of Kurds—

52

and they have all concurred that the bag is mine!"

When I heard this nonsense I said to the judge, "Your Honour, do not let your judgement be blurred by the absurd words of this dastardly Kurd! That bag is mine and *I* can tell you what's inside. It has—

a house in ruins

a school for boys

a dog kennel

four chess players

tents and tentpoles

the city of Basra

the city of Baghdad

the ancient palace of Shaddad ibn-Aad

a smithy's forge

a shepherd's crook

a fishing net

five handsome boys

twelve delightful girls

and one thousand leaders of caravans—

and every single one of them will tell you the bag is mine!"

The Kurd burst into tears. He said, "Most honourable magistrate, do not let your mind be misled by the malice of this mendacious Middle Eastern merchant! The bag is mine and it contains—

a stone fort

with fourteen towers

thirty-two alchemical powers

four men playing chess

a mare and a stallion and a newborn foal

a lance

a rabbit

a roaring lion

three kings from the east

two courtesans
and a comedian
a rabbi with two cantors
a priest with two deacons
a mullah with two servants
a captain with two sailors
an honest man with two liars
and a cadi with two witnesses—
and both of them will swear and testify that the bag is mine!"

When I heard this nonsense my fury rose to my nostrils (and believe me, O Commander of the Faithful, it hurt to have my fury rise to my nostrils), and I cried out, "O Judge, the bag is mine and only mine. It contains—

lotions and potions
philtres and enchantments
miracles and wonders
shades and phantoms
a garden with figs and apples
grapes and vines
whispers and cries
murmurs and sighs
nibbles and giggles
two lovers rising from their bed
a loud blast from behind
two quiet poofies
plus *rahatlokoum*
and *babaghanoush*
and *imambaldi*
and green eggs and ham
and *baklava*
and toasted pita
and a parade with drums and banners
flags and flutes and singers and dancers
and a man playing the clarinet
and a plank

and a nail
and a thousand *dinars*
and the city of Kufah
and the city of Gaza
and the old library behind the plaza
and it also contains
all of the land that stretches
from Cairo to Jerusalem to Damascus to the Middle Kingdom
to Isfahan
in addition to which my bag contains
a foolish shopkeeper
a sleepless Caliph
a brave girl
a wise granny
a silent prince
a warrior who fights without swords
plus the sun and the moon and darkness and rain
and a human heart
and seven old men
and a curious traveller
and a sick princess
and a quick bird
and a primrose
and two soldiers
and a blue butterfly
and a little boy who ponders big riddles
and a father who wishes he had more answers
and an angry king
and a tall fiddler
and a short storyteller
and happy listeners
and loud clapping
and more loud clapping
and it also has in it
a coffin

a shroud

and a razor for the beard of the cadi—

if he does not agree the bag belongs to me!"

The judge looked puzzled as he listened to our recital. He said, "Either the two of you are making fun of the law and its representative, or this bag is as deep as the Abyss and as all-encompassing as the Day of Judgement itself. I see that I shall have to open the bag and see for myself what it contains." And he opened the bag and looked inside.

And the father said to his little boy, "What do you think
the bag contains?"

— And that, your Majesty, is the end of my story.

— That is not a good place to stop your story, Storyteller! You
haven't told me what the father told the little boy Ali the Persian told
the Caliph Haroun al-Rashid the judge found inside the bag! You've
left everything in suspense.

— I cannot tell you the rest, your Majesty, because I do not
know how this story ends. You see, I am the father in my story and
my own son is the little boy. I was telling him that story of Ali the
Persian tonight when your guard came to summon me to your
presence. I had just asked my son the question, "What do you think
the bag contains?" when I was interrupted and had to leave. His
answer would have given me the ending of my story. If I had known
I would never see my son again, I would have given the story my
own ending—but what person knows the hour of their own death?
... Not even you, your Majesty, not even you.

— If you die tonight you will never hear your son's answer.

— Well, perhaps he will become a storyteller himself one day, and tell his answer to a new listener.

— Storyteller ... My good, wise spinner of tales, you will not die tonight. You will go home and you will hear your son's answer. Let your return be the tenth story you promised him, and let it have a happy ending. You have shown me tonight what had been hidden from me. The teller and the tale are one and cannot be separated, for each shelters the other. Perhaps only Worldmaker knows the last word in our story, not kings ... or storytellers.

— You are merciful, your Majesty.

— By the way, what *did* the judge find inside that bag?

— What do *you* think, O King?

— Oh ... probably just a few olive pits, a dried crust of bread, an orange rind ... and a story.

— Yes, that's exactly what he found! And when Ali the Persian heard this he laughed and said, "Oh, well ... it probably wasn't mine after all." And when the Caliph Haroun al-Rashid heard the story the pain was lifted from his heart, and he laughed and laughed and laughed.

SOURCES AND ACKNOWLEDGEMENTS

The story about how death came into the world, in "The Last Story," is retold from the story "Tortoises, Men and Stones," from *The Origin of Life and Death*, ed. Ulli Beier, by permission of the publisher, Heinemann Publishers (Oxford) Ltd.

The story of the soul wandering in the form of a bumblebee or butterfly, in "The Dreamer and the Butterfly," is traditional in many northern countries. Versions can be found in Scandinavian, Icelandic, and English collections. I particularly enjoy the story of "The Dreamer and the Treasure" in *Icelandic Folktales and Legends*, Jacqueline Simpson (London: B.T. Batsford Ltd.).

"The Green Mist" is my modern version of a story collected by Mrs. Balfour and published in 1891 in *Folk-Lore* (vol. II, September, 1891, "Legends of the Cars"). I took the liberty of bringing the story into the language of my own time and place, although I enjoyed sounding out the thick Lincolnshire dialect in which it was originally told and recorded. Both Alan Garner and Kevin Crossley-Holland have used this tale in collections of, respectively, goblin stories and English stories.

"The True Father of the House" is a Norwegian story. My telling is based on a translation into English by G.W. Dasent published in 1874. My thanks to the staff of The Osborne Collection, Toronto Public Library, for their help in locating a public domain version on which to base my telling. A fine modern translation has been published by Pat Shaw and Carl Norman in *Norwegian Folktales* (New York: Pantheon).

"The Bird Colour-of-Time" is freely translated from Jocelyn Bérubé's tale "L'Oiseau Couleur du Temps," which is his original take on a traditional motif. It was recorded on his album *Nil en Ville* (Montreal, 1976). I gratefully acknowledge his permission to let me retell his story in English and in my own way.

"How Heart Came into the World" is based on my memory of a Ugandan story called "The Creation of the World," which I read many years ago in a book titled *African Myths and Folktales*, ed. Charlotte and Wolf Leslau (White Plains: Peter Pauper Press, 1963). I gratefully acknowledge the publisher's permission to let me retell the story here.

"The Master of the Tea Ceremony" is my free translation from Pascal Fauliot's book *Les Contes des Arts Martiaux* (Paris: Editions Retz). I gratefully acknowledge his permission to let me retell this story in English.

"The Silent Prince" was inspired by a story titled "The Mute Princess" in Howard Schwartz's *Elijah's Violin and Other Jewish Fairy Tales* (New York: Harper and Row). My story shares with his the motif of a silent character who is told riddles and thus drawn into speech. My first dilemma story is adapted from "Who Cured the Princess?" a story recorded by Moshe Kaplan as heard from a Polish rabbi (Israel Folktale Archives 464); collected in *Folktales of Israel*, ed. Dov Noy (Chicago: University of Chicago Press). The second story was sent to me by Carol McDougal, who heard it from a Portuguese girl recently arrived in Toronto from her village in the Azores. Carol was a children's librarian at the time, and the girl told her story at the library's story hour. The third dilemma story uses the well-known motif of the seal-wife, and mixes it with stories I have heard from Cree and Iroquois friends about the beings they call Thunderbirds. In the western wonder tale tradition, it seems to me these thunder-beings are close cousins to the Firebird.

"Ali the Persian's Bag" comes from the best-known story collection in the world: *The Thousand Nights and One Night*, aka the *Arabian Nights*. I have borrowed from both Payne and Burton translations, and couldn't resist adding a little spice of my own.

I have made every effort to trace and seek permission from the copyright holders of stories that are not in the public domain, and that serve as sources for the versions in The Storyteller at Fault. *I would be grateful if any errors or omissions were pointed out, so that they may be corrected.*   D.Y.

KAREN BLACKWOOD

DAN YASHINSKY

regularly performs and travels, and has been active in The Storytellers School of Toronto. He says: "The stories that came together to make this book are all ones I like to tell. I've always loved 'frame-stories' like *The Canterbury Tales*, the *Decameron*, and the *Arabian Nights*; this is my take on this venerable device of oral literature." *The Storyteller at Fault* was first performed at the Tarragon Theatre's Extra Space in Toronto in 1991, with original music by Oliver Schroer. Dan Yashinsky's first book, *Tales for An Unknown City* (McGill-Queen's University Press), was published in 1990 and was shortlisted for the City of Toronto Book Prize.

GREG HENDERSON

NANCY CAIRINE PITT

studied privately and at the Ontario College of Art. In 1979 she showed a ten-year retrospective of her paintings at Galerie la Murée in Montreal. Her work is in many private collections. She has travelled and lived in Europe, and lived for many years in Quebec. She now makes her home in Prince Edward Island.